OMEGA'S GUMBO

OMEGA MCNEAL

Library of Congress Control Number: 2025912967
Orders by U.S. trade bookstores and wholesalers.

ISBN: 978-1-966612-36-0

Cover Design: amman_wpdesign

Veronica Miller, Red Diamond Editing by V. Rena,

reddiamondediting5@yahoo.com

First Printed Edition July 2025

Printed in the United States of America

OMEGA'S MENU

THE TABLE IS SET: CONTENTS

Chapter I: Grace Goodness

God said, "In the beginning, the Word was God, and God was the Word." I thank God for blessing me with the gift of spoken word. This chapter begins Omega's Gumbo by blessing the substance for your soul.

Chapter II: Layers of Life

This chapter represents that space where you can't find understanding, wondering how you got here. It's that space where options feel limited and your back is against the wall. It's the space where your strength is made perfect only through God. You know He gave you the gift to write your way out.

Chapter III: Sexy Spices

Passion and desire drive me, and I am free to express how I want to touch, feel, and make love or lust. What are you in the mood for, without judgment? I say faithfully to these sheets, simply because they respect my *PEN*etration.

Chapter IV: Pitch of Patience

Love thy neighbor as thyself. Where in life did this die? Once upon a time, we were a village looking out for one another. Now, we are our own worst enemy, seeking to kill, hate, and destroy one another. I am my sister's keeper and my brother's backbone. My heart is a place the world can call *home*. May these words be the welcome mat for change.

Chapter V: Sweet and Sour

Love is a vacant move, next to the lie that got you evicted. My mind has left you, and my body has mutated into a shell of the woman you once knew. Not even the salt from my tears could preserve the love I once knew.

Chapter VI: Light My Fire

Love has warmed the hearts of many, to fuel future understanding and to create the foundation for you and me. If you have not loved, you have not lived. **God is love**, and through Him, we love one another in so many different ways.

Chapter VII: Omega's Oven

360 degrees will complete anything that life will dish out. Omega is the end of many new beginnings. May God bless and thank you for your support of a
Hungry Poet!

MINOR MINOR

I watch the seconds count down,
The microwave clicks my plate.
I anticipate, I can't wait,
To feed this beast inside me no one can see.
My plate piled high, no one knows why,
I put on so much weight.
In my mind, she says, *Eat and you* will *feel better,*
All the time, like a song.
I eat bread burdens,
I figure, heavy load for heavy loads.
I get it—it's because I'm tired of everyone,
Watching me swell.
Who I am anymore, I can't tell,
I was a 7 and now a 14.
To bigger women, this is nothing,
But like my problem, I'm not used to carrying this.
My grocery list consists of:
12 dozen issues,
6 rolls of tissues,
10 pounds of situations,
A family pack of problems *Sweet 'n' Low* can't solve.

Only to be told, *Just stop eating or eat less,*
If this was a test, I fail,
As my belly swells and my thighs grow thicker,
Simply because I had a buffet of why's.
Is there sunshine in slimmer waistlines?
Then why are bulimics empty,
And overeating never fills souls?
In life, with too much on my plate,
What is my fate?
A size satisfied with self—
I wear it well.

OPPRESS NO MORE

They carrying on about the world is a juggle,
And you aren't living—just surviving.
They are trying to pull me down, but I'm still gliding.
Then I realize from slant eyes they were high,
High on that gossip, that good shit.
I told them they need to quit.
They tried to get me on it,
Talking about, *Did you hear about that one?*
While trying to blow my mind like a gun.
I said I'm good, cause I'm a poet,
And I can inhale thoughts, sniff similes.
Methyl metaphors, pimp participles to all lyrical hoes,
Tap dance puppet poets and get ready for this.
Lyrist drive pen through wrist just to bleed this *POETRY,*
And I will write until my soul is sore,
Because I'm not gonna be oppressed no more.
Back bends, bones ache, shake me up, but I won't break,
While skin lighter than mine sit and recline.
I'm told, *Be respectful* by saying, *I am fine,*
I'm laying low through my complete being.

To the European who told me affirmative action,
Is reverse discrimination.
Yet never a conversation,
About stealing a whole nation.
And reparations are as equal,
As the sweeter substitutes—
A sugar box of hard knock life's sweet and low.
The aftertaste in my mouth as bitter,
As the Confederate flag of the South.
Yet, I know who I am to know what I know,
And I'm not gonna be oppressed no more.

I KNOW WHAT IT'S LIKE

I know what it's like—
I know what it's like to want to fly,
But it seems your wings were clipped at birth,
I know what it's like to question your worth.
I know what it's like for your ears to hear,
Someone else knows your fears,
But they've never been there.
Here in a cage, Maya's bird still sings,
I know what it's like to question the future God brings.
I know what it's like to have winter instead of spring,
I know what it's like to look forward to warm summers,
Only to fall back into the cold world.
You got me slipping, tripping, sliding,
And fighting a war of fiction—
Battling with my own ambitions.
Wishing to know what it's like,
To be dry, to try without the storms of harm,
To rain away the Divine light.
I know what it's like—
To keep sight of what's right,
Thrown from innocence.

My repentance, life I'm forgiven,
Only life's not willing.
To move the past,
To clear the path for someone to see the present.
Ignored alone, in a room crowded but not excited,
Life's war, I battle with self,
Wondering when peace left.
To be with our backs against the wall,
My space is tight.

Danesha and Dakota—
I know what it's like.
March 8, 1994, Rest in Peace

MY AIR

Toni said it best,
When she said she will never breathe again—
Breathe again, no, no, no, baby,
Now I'm still waiting to exhale.
Listen to me close,
Listen to the story that I tell.
You were my life, my world, my air,
All I ever, ever wanted was for you to be there.
To show me, baby, that you care.
I gave you my all, my life to share,
'Cause you were my air.
My love for you was never appreciated,
My life was completely dedicated—
To loving you.
But it's hard work loving someone,
Who isn't worth your time.
You were a heart crusher,
A game player.
Just corruption to my mind,
You made it believable to me,
That there is a thin line.

I hate you more than I ever loved you from the start,
One day, you will see that,
you should have done right by me.
Now you see the happiness I brought someone else,
You know you regret the day that you left.
It is hard for you to see someone taking your place,
But, baby, remember the pain you left on my face.

LET GO

Don't hold back,
We can take it slow,
Put your heart in me and let go.
I can be more than you will ever need,
More than you can ever know,
Don't hold back—let your feelings go.
You got your guard up,
With a wall between us.
What will it take to have you completely?
What will it take to gain your trust?
Your trust is a must,
Or there is *no* us,
And I want us to be together.
Will I let you go?
Baby, never.
I want to be with you now and infinity,
Because it is me for you and you for me,
This is the way it should be.
And all I ask you to do is...

Stop pushing me away,
Not letting me close to you.
Putting me in a state of confusion,
Leaving me not knowing what to do.
I speak the truth whenever three words are spoken,
Give me your heart—it will never be broken.
I can't love you more than you will ever know,
Don't hold back emotion,
Baby, just let go.

MY VERSE

Sometimes, I feel like a blank verse,
An untitled curse or, worse, a poet without a purpose.
I feel less than—a pen with no ink, worthless,
Too many times, I'm only worth the lines I rhyme,
That's why I do this.
My soul swings on a pendulum that crosses paths—
Life laughs when my sanity cries,
And serenity sobs—
Opportunity without doorknobs, emptiness.
Poetry plugs pain, potholes on the daily—
Poor man's therapy, keeping me from crazy.
My poetry signs checks when the rent's due.
She writes prescriptions for life's flu.
Poetry becomes crayons,
When I'm a thousand shades blue.
A paintbrush to draw feathers on eagle's wings,
A pen to sketch in better things.

Poetry is my child support bond for court,
A bandage for the hurt,
My job when I had no work.
My only friend when I'm surrounded by foes,
The answer to shit I don't know,
The fertilizer when my progress won't grow.
A jumper cable for a car that won't start,
A witness to my broken heart.
Elevation when I feel so low,
The harvest when it seems my seeds won't grow.
Mama when I was lonely,
Daddy when he didn't want to be.
Sister when family faded,
That voice who said, "You can make it."
Poetry is my lover when others would cheat,
Comforter when I couldn't sleep.
Poetry was the telephone when I thought God wasn't listening,
My twinkling star for everything I'm wishing.
Danielle, lady of Daniel,
I, too, have been in the lion's den.
Omega is the beginning that won't ever end.
Chambliss comes from Chambliss, fine French wine—
It's like my poetry; I pour all of me every time I rhyme.
Danielle Omega Chambliss defines me
Into the poetry I write, recite.
It is my light,
And every time I rhyme,
I'm going to let it shine, let it shine.

I'm the word, and the word is me.
Poetry is scripture,
And I am a living verse.
I didn't write poetry—
She wrote me first.

CHOCOLATE COVERED ANGEL

God kissed the earth and gave birth to a chocolate-covered angel,
And made his wings like an eagle—
Every time he holds me, my heart soars,
And every time he is near me, my cat roars.
In his presence, I crave him—
My double-dose deluxe, in that touch, I want more.
I awake to beautiful mornings,
Where tulips are wet with morning dew.
And my two lips stay moistened,
with just thoughts of you.
While I rest on his chest,
Pop quiz—he puts my body to the test.
I confess, I enjoy looking into his almond-colored windows,
Draped with curved eyelashes.
I see reflections of our passion,
All the time, do we play.
Every day, a new mystery with my love—
Trust, he knows how to treat her.

Yet, we have had our times—
Times I've said even the devil was a beautiful angel.
Deception was killed by trust,
And my lifelong trinity of the God in he and me.
God, man, and woman come together,
We write our names in the sand,
Putting God first in our plan.
I can listen to the time capsule,
That beats the sound of all that he is worth—
Just to remember that God kissed the earth and gave birth.

SOMEBODY SAVE OUR BABIES

Somebody save our babies,
This world gone crazy,
Men not being men, just boys being lazy.
No fathers to the baby,
God bless the motherless child.
That feels he has no one,
Let Thy will be done.
Stories never told,
When they took their child's soul,
Many times, I've been told.
"You're never gonna make it,"
Quick, do the Lord giveth fast—
Do He takes it?
Nobody knows the hour or the minute,
That your body will be separated from your spirit.

Growing up, knowing everything,
They don't want to hear it.
There is no reality of the pain,
That we put each other through,
When we do what we do.
We can't understand why,
Things are the way they are,
Or have to be,
I guess this will never make sense to me.
A mother's heavy heart is a heavy load,
A child is a treasure worth more than its weight in gold.
When will we learn?
Instead, we earn tomb to tomb,
And abortions rock babies to sleep,
Before their first heartbeat—
Death in the womb.
Now people question why society is doomed.
That's why I think the world gone crazy,
Somebody save our babies.
I thought somebody cursed my first step,
Until I understood why Jesus wept.
Yet, I kept asking why problems keep coming,
And then started wishing,
That it stopped, being brighter days that we're missing.
Lord, so many times I call on Your name,
And when we meet again, *my will* will never be the same.

They took prayer out of schools,
And wonder why we break the rules.
Kids trading their ambition for ammunition,
To shoot away their dreams and goals.
So many things we want that we can't have,
The price we pay, so many pushing up daisies,
Somebody save our babies.

MY DIVINE

My divine light, my divine light,
When adversaries utter criticizing sound,
My light won't let me drown.
My divine light, my divine light.
When chaos and corruption sweep the earth,
Peace be still in your face,
So, there is where I hold sight.
Two days old and already my heart flutters for direction,
For you, what to do.
I look into your face and God's Divine Intervention,
Pours through.
Issues today, answers come tomorrow.
My divine light, her scent pure, face complete, essence shallow,
Only to regurgitate your fate and happiness.
I can't explain,
No one could understand when I looked at you that,
Just had to be your name—
My Divine Light, My Divine Light,

I pray God will give me insight,
To raise you to shine.
By His grace, we make decisions with an open mind.
My princess brings bliss with your first step, straight spine.
Partners for life, spiritual umbilical cord in the Lord,
Forever through time.
Spiritual tears come from the miracles of birth,
Bringing forth light.
I thank God for my Divine Light.

HOLDING WISDOM

I conceived knowledge a long time ago.
Carrying all the information to know better.
It wasn't until I had to push through the lies and insecurities that
I learned to be better.
Your face was the reflection of letting go.
I hold you tighter to apply what I already know.
I am strong and so are you.
We have the stripes for all we been through.
Your essence gave me strength to straighten my spine.
I walk upright, head up, not wasting time.
I pray I can be someone you can be proud of, for never settling,
Never accepting just anything,
Holding on to you, what joy you bring, know I choose you.
God chose me to be your mother, steward to guide you to better.
Better than your grandmother's mama.
Guide you to a life of peace not drama.
Confidence, not doubt, self-love, self-awareness,
Roar loud, my lioness,
Never let them silence your greatness.
They are not enough, if they think you too much,
Walk in excellence and finish what you touch.

My Wisdom is loving you to infinity.
Lord, help me make her better than me.
Keep your crown straight, polish, and never sit it down.
You are the child of the King, always know I hold you dear to my heart,
Holding Wisdom gave me a new start.

SLAUGHTER HOUSE

Secret sins, send lost saints to stay in slaughterhouses.
And the door has a welcome mat that has been turned upside down as
they entered the room. How did they arrive?
They don't know how,
God is calling you, but you ignore the sound.
The windows are decorated with last year's drapes.
Blocking the sun from shining brighter better tomorrow's.
Hidden behind many blind sorrows, the floor has footprints that run in.
circles,
The dust mites delight in the misery of many, the stored mirrors.
I can see everyone else but me burning my conscience.

"Keep the fireplace lit," God whispers again.
I can't hear you. I can't feel it, it burns my conscience.
Only the Holy Spirit can heal it. Scream, send chills.
I'm wrapped up in His arms.

It's not hot enough lite, lighters near my lips, not hot enough so I drink,
drinks that warm my insides.
Only I'm still cold the slaughterhouse, how did I get here?
I was left feeling brought or sold.
My Messiah labeled me priceless.

Now, I just need to believe it.

RANDOMNESS

Randomness, all over the place to only be nowhere.

My body is not my own. My thoughts remind me it is on loan.

Split two poles, too high to be bipolar or bilingual, speaking flesh and
spirit.

My flesh says *murder, destroy, kill*; my spirit says, *lift love and build.*

Randomness, I eat off everybody's plate, but my mind never understands.

How am I so full yet?

Starvin', craving tattoos of tomorrow's to cover up today's scars.

I find freedom in these bars.

I'll write these love letters to my demons, asking them nicely to divorce
me, Murder married us a long time ago.

I was an accomplice or the accessory.

I look...

Her right in the eyes, watching her soul leave her body, fall to her knees,

Asking God, why did an innocent have to die?

Why is she on my conscience? My silence is a lie.

I've tried to testify on stages. In stages, God is my witness.

I don't get none of this.

A producer, not helpin' me water disease.

There were dull green thumbs, black-and-blue eyes close.

But I see you just to have the seas judge the tree.

My babies have become strange fruit.
It's hard to recognize one whose smile is incarcerated. With you.
Ipad, uh, her happiness, brothers and sisters sent away.
Still finding strength to help her plan out your Father's Day.
The other has wrote me off as an emotional liability.
My apologies can never create new blueprints.
Just prayers sent, who are the most high to create stronger foundations.
Salvation solidified.
Sanity sand that is always quick to sink into generational curses.
For my children, I will be our generational rock climber.
Refusing to let them sink in the quicksand,
Of past mistakes. I would rather take the fall before I settled for
complacency.
Your crowns are at stake. Never leave your throne for him to sit in your
lap.
He can take his place as king or I'll just leave him to the peasants.
Let the Bible be the blueprint to how you rule your Queendom.

SHOWER OF PAIN

Baby, baby, I'm just thinking of you,
And all the things that we useta do.
Why did you leave me, leave me this way?
When I asked you what was wrong, *nothing* you would say.
Many storms and chills of the rain,
Laying here thinking in my shower,
My shower of pain.
Now I see, I see the loss,
And being hurt is my biggest cost.
Baby, I know we are through,
But I'm so sorry for what I did to you.
I useta wake up in the morning with you by my side,
Pain comes as our love slowly died.
Nights I long to touch your face,
I know it is too late, but I'll admit the mistake.
Because, baby, I'm ashamed,
Laying here thinking in my shower,
My shower of pain.
Ooh baby, I want to say what is done is done,
Because you are the only one,
That can make me feel the way I do.

If you come back to me,
There is nothing I won't do.
To make you see and understand,
You and I are part of God's perfect plan.
In my heart, you will always be near,
My love for you shall remain.
Laying here thinking in my shower,
My shower of pain.

BABY FORGIVE ME

Baby, forgive me,
Baby, I'm sorry.
For all I've done,
Because you are the only one.
You're the only one that could touch my heart;
I'm begging you for a new start.
Let's start all over again,
I lost my baby; I lost my best friend.
Baby, I didn't realize your love was real,
It was hard for me to show you how I feel.
Now that you are gone, I feel I can't move on,
I wish I hadn't ever left you alone.
Good things are never missed until they're gone.
Now I know no one can love me the way you do,
I can't change the past, but I wish I knew—
I wish I knew then, what I know now.
I don't know how I let you go,
Baby, I know.
All I know is...

Forgive me, please,
Because you're all I ever need,
To love me.
Let's go back to the way we useta be.
Can you forgive me?

WHY WASN'T IT MEANT TO BE?

Many say it wasn't meant to be.
That is what many have told me,
You were the light in my eyes.
I was blind to the fact and could not see,
I was blind and could not see the way I was being used.
I mistook love for lust because I was so confused,
Trying to love you was just confusion to my reality;
It was never meant to be.
Why couldn't it be me for you, and you for me?
The reason, I can't see,
Why it was never meant to be?
I let my guard down
And was completely open toward you.
There's nothing in my life,
To someday be your wife,
And live happily ever after.
But that could only happen,

In the land of make-believe,
Because you're pushing me away from your reality.
And I don't understand why,
It wasn't meant to be.
Why couldn't it be me for you,
And you for me?
The reason, I can't see,
Why it was never meant to be?

EVERLASTING LOVE

Everlasting love is what you've given to me,
You're the joy of my reality,
Every hour of the day, I have thoughts of you.
I sit and think about what you do to me,
This love should last forever,
Now and for eternity.
You're the song in my heart,
That makes me sing,
About our... Oh, this sweet love,
Could only come from my God above.
I swear I never knew a love like this,
Only God knows because He is my witness.
Our love is inseparable,
Our love can't be broken.
Since the day three words were spoken.
You greet me with a kiss and with a smile,
Killer passionate love to make our bodies go wild.
Because, baby, you're my all, you're my everything,
'Cause we have that everlasting love.
This is what you've given to me.
You're the joy of my reality.

WHY ME?

I can't see what I did,
To deserve this.
I can't see, I can't see,
Why me, baby, why me?
Is this something that I caused myself?
Why is it every time I look around,
I'm the only one left?
I ask myself, why me?
Am I the only one that can see
That all I want is to love?
I never wanted to desert you.
All I wanted was to be there.
You pushed me away.
When I asked what was wrong,
Nothing, you would say,
I drown in my tears, my body's wrapped with pain,
All I wanted was you to love me the same.
Now I'm so lonely; who can I blame?
Left with so much pain and misery,
I ask myself, why me?

Because I never tried so hard to keep someone,
Who didn't want to be kept.
When you left me, baby,
Did you think how I felt?
Nobody will ever understand,
Why I love that man.
He hurt me once; I let him hurt me again,
My mind is gone; I don't know where it all started,
I just remember when it ended.
I'm stupid for loving you,
Stupid for caring.
Stupid for sharing my life, it was a waste,
But no one will ever take your place.
Slowly, as my heart dies,
You could never apologize.
For what you did to me.
I ask myself, why me?

SANITY SYMPHONY

Stepping stones surround serenity,
Secretly snatching my sanity today.
Heart-filled soul sits, half-past right and wrong.
I am a walk instrumental of misery's theme song.
I try to change the notes.
Life keeps kicking me in the throat,
I try to change the melody,
By not letting life get to me.
I will make my own music,
My own poetic symphony.
Conducting pep rallies, chanting,
"I can do it; it's going to get better,"
I never let her look back at me and sing the blues.
I refuse to dance off beat to survival's defeat.
Every time the choir sings, "Trouble don't last always,"
I'm going through—if only you knew.
My poetry is the glue that holds me,
Consoles me, told me.
I no longer have to listen to misery's tune,

I can write my own song for life, where flowers bloom.

I presume, proclaim, and predicate that I won't break,

I'm a Pisces; I don't swim with the guppies—self-pity is a lake.

I will never drown; I'm lifted up because God holds me down.

Hear the sound of a dollar piece—Pisces, two fish, one sign,

Blow my mind—the creation of positive portraits,

Painted into my po-ality.

Poetry meets reality,

Holding me together through thin or thick.

I walk with a big Bic or split slick similes,

Symphonies that smooth me.

When my back is against the wall, and the cry for help—

No one answers the call to be close to the Creator of us,

In God, I trust.

And like He that is in me, I rise again.

Battle scars hurt while metaphors mend.

Poetic prescriptions filled to cure what I'm feeling—

Similes smooth pain in haiku healing.

Anytime I reveal what I'm feeling, like:

She was 11 years old with a story never told,

About starvation sitting next to her sanity,

With the audacity to stand up and tell me,

She is too broke for anyone to pay attention.

Even mention the bruises that life chooses to place on her—

Like college payment plans, her dream will defer,

Until she can pay the fee to be free.

Pandora's Box of the hard knocks was her last gift,

It was wrapped with ribbons of despair.
Lead covered her dreams, destiny duct-taped her fate,
While hopelessness silenced her screams.
Sadly, she never ever asked you to care,
But this piece is to let you know she is there—
There, where steppingstones surround serenity,
Secretly snatching sanity today.

THE TEARS NEVER SEEN

My tears never seen,
My cries never heard.
My pains in the shadows,
My mind becomes idle now due to circumstance.
Why was I never given a chance to know?
As a child, why was I exiled from my family?
Was it even meant for me?
To grab hope as a handkerchief—
What I wouldn't give to wake up,
Without a problem.
360° makes a revolution,
Which is the solution—it symbolizes complete.
The truth in what I speak.
Bless the scripture,
Words painting pictures.
Lyrical artist—pretty pictures I paint into your mental,
Make it monumental to the knowledge absorbed.
May God be my guide and the Bible my sword.
Not always do I walk the straight and narrow.
I'm a queen and kids.

If my tears were seen, would they be wiped away?
I'm tired of hearing lies about the brighter days.
Why give birth if we can't treasure what a life is really worth?
Do you know what I mean?

WHEN MY HEART CRIES

In my life, a silver spoon I lose or never had.
Situation sad when the future seems fictitious,
Non-existent to us.
I sit and reminisce about,
Our ancestors—given little but could do plenty,
Now we are given much, only to become greedy.
My heart cries, my eyes close,
To see a future that only God knows.
My heart cries again,
When I see the end with no beginning.
Like life quickly ends before it begins—
Gone before the start,
Only to live and still have it hard.
Once again, why?
An endless question,
Making the mental confession to not wonder,
And moving.
I've got to always try,
Even when my heart cries.

MIND

I got to Keep a Meditation,
I close my eyes to go somewhere far.
When they open, I am dancing with a star.
Housing with the planets,
Swinging with the universe,
Caught a poetation in my verse.
I close my eyes and hide in my poetry,
Power in my pen won't let you get to me.
Closing my eyes once more, I see stars,
Behind bars, plead no contest to accessory.
When my third eye is blind by a polluted society,
Why, oh why, why, why?
My memory bank is in overdraft,
Because I can't remember the right path,
The devils after me, but God will have the last laugh.

I got a meditation,
There is power in the poetry,
So I grab a pen and take my medication.
Fill the page in rage,
Take verbs instead of herb—slow not to overdose.
I chine a rhythm line; this is verbal fine,
Instead of powder, just another white devil to the mind.
Closing my eyes once again,
I reunite with just an old friend,
It's my pad and my pen.
We keep writing for old time's sake.
I write away my problems, troubles, and blue.
I erase away the mistake,
Cross out hate and write in my fate.
Sailing in the sea as the wind blows, don't pity me.
Set my sails high to catch opportunity.
The captain of the ship is the only one that knows,
Even behind prison bars, your mind can still grow.
Closing my eyes one last time,
To disappear to a place so good,
It stays in mind.

NOT SAID

Something Left Unsaid,
How many thoughts of you run through my head?
Too blind to see what is right in front of me,
It was fiction in my reality,
As to what you really mean to me.
How much do you mean to me? It's hard to say.
I just know for you I care.
In your presence, happiness comes,
When you're gone, I'm left wishing you were there.
There's a smile in your name that comes,
To my face every time it is said.
You may never know,
How many thoughts of you run through my head?
Why can't I tell you? I am a woman with no voice,
My heart has been scattered to give; I have no choice.
Because I have little to give,
But yet, I can tell you, I am with no voice.
I see you, but with me, completely, this may never be said.
Yet, in my silence to confess what I feel, I can't say,
But I dread the fact of letting you slip away.

If you reach your hand, I will take it,
And the way you will lead,
Away from the games, the truth will set me free.

DO MY WANTS AND NEEDS MATTER?

Do my wants and needs matter?
Relationships don't seem to get better.
Will I ever discover a good brother—
To be special to me and love me,
And fulfill my every need?
He won't neglect my wants.
I'm searching high and low to find such a man.
He will say, "What do you want? And what do you need?"
He'll make everything come to reality.
But now it seems everybody's out for self,
Their feelings and emotions cared about, and nobody else's.
So now, the question I ask,
As time passes, do my wants and needs really matter?
Do my wants and needs matter?
Relationships don't seem to get better.
When I was younger, I used to chase a man.
Now I'm older, and I realize that I don't give a damn.
They say men are not all the same,
But how can I separate the truth from a game?

What I wouldn't give to be in the loving arms of a stranger—
But I'm willing to risk putting my mind, body, and soul in danger.
I don't know if I can, baby, I can't.
My soul's growing weak, my heart's getting faint.
And then the question you ask,
What do you want?
As time passes, what do you need?
Help me see,
That they matter.

HE SPEAK

God looks at the intentions of your heart
And the methods of your mind.
But have you ever felt, sometimes,
That God looks at you with His eyes closed?
Yet, only He knows the tears in the shadows,
The weeps in the whispers of that space—
The space between conviction and conscience.
In that space right there, a deaf debate begins,
To blow breath onto a wasted existence
That finds fault in friends but no foundation of self.
Preacher purpose, preacher purpose,
In a parable that she can't grasp.
She laughs at her own reflection,
Then has her own reconciliation.
She said, "I said I am going to be somebody.
I am going to do something with myself 30 years ago."
What do you know, epiphany?
Sometimes, I feel God looks at me,
With His eyes closed.

Yet, only He knows the tears in the shadows,
The weeps in the whispers—
Debating conviction versus conscience.
Jesus speaks.

SOLDIER OF LOVE

Clocks tick, keeper of time.
My heart catches, occupies the space in my mind.
I smile in my sleep because, in my dreams, we meet.
I can't wait to walk through the mirrors of your eyes,
Down the hallway of your heart where my soul rests.
Although to get here, you and I have been through many tests,
Nevertheless, I know I am blessed.
Because there are scriptures that beat in your chest,
Revelation in your lips,
And prophecies in your fingertips.
I know because every time you touch me, I am fulfilled.
And this is real—for once, this is not a game.
My heart anticipates the day I take your name,
Simply because he accepts all of me completely,
No matter who I am, was, or will be.
For me, my confidence says *I'm* the one, always first,
While my conscience has made me question my worth.
I am a dollar piece, Pisces—I swim in both directions.
You have heard my heart sing my inner confession.
You did it, made it through every maze, booby trap, Ft. Knox,
My own National Guard.
Because it takes a real soldier to capture my heart.
I surrender.

LORD, I PRAY

Lord, I pray in an amazing way,
You will come into my life.
Grab me by the hand and lead me away,
From confusion, battles, losing situations, tribulation, and strife.
Lord, I pray for healing—
To not hold it in but revealing what I am feeling.
Lord, I pray for heart conviction,
To cast out demons like crack addiction, past infliction.
To send up prayers and no longer wishing, but now knowing,
In Your way, to continue growing.
Through me, let faith start showing.
I stand on my foundation—
God first to my dedication.
'Cause Lord, I pray for:
That baby who won't stop crying,
That politician who won't stop lying,
The mother who won't stop trying,
The sons and daughters who won't stop dying,
The addict who won't stop buying,
The terrorists who won't stop flying,
For that opportunity to stop denying.

Lord, I pray for the handle to close doors—
To hopelessness, poverty, and scandal.
Lord, I pray for You to be the way maker.
Thank You for not being the forsake,
Lord, I pray for words to lift weights,
Power in the tongue to move evil, suffering, and hate.
Lord, I pray to cast care and lift things off my shoulders.
God, You say I am more than a conqueror—
In Your word, I know it.
For it is written:
Blessed are the POET.
AMEN.

MISS YOU

I'm that money piece, Pisces—two fish on one sign, 29.
I'm older than three of my oldest brothers,
Who all died before 25.
Life leaking tears every time reality cracks.
Sanity sober, serenity seals—
Broken dreams in the windows of life.
Shed tears to cleanse the windows like raindrops,
Drizzle your past, moisten memories.
Skeletons shake, slivering secrets become damp,
Shed a tear to warm forgotten souls.
I celebrate living while I'm mourning the leaving,
They left in 6-feet-deep cracks of my reality.
Pottery to poetry—every verse I let mold me,
To be a mental chess player, checkmate.
'Til I make you think about the ones you're missing.

SISTA'S KEEPER

Am I my sista's keeper?
I'm the foundation if problems get deeper.
The shoulder to cry on when he don't need her,
The clip in the 9 if he thinks he wants to beat her.
I'm child support when it's due,
Making men fathers who don't have a clue.
See, I am my sista's keeper—
God's the bond; I'm the glue,
Brother, I thought you knew.
It's that God in me to be my sista's keeper.
As we have shed tears when husbands are cheating.
Boyfriends are BS feeding,
And self-esteem has evaporated.
That's why I'm dedicated to being my sista's keeper.
When babies are denied, mothers have cried,
Fathers have lied, I've tried—
Constantly to be my sista's keeper.
Yes, I am,
Forgive me if I give a damn.

BLACK MAN

Black man is a man that has had it hard for oh so long,
That's why he has to be strong.
Where are all our good Black men?
I guess out trying to make a dollar quicker.
Little kids growing up want to be a big dope dealer.
People have their minds on their money and their money on their minds,
Don't mean to take each other out with guns and nines.
Yet, you can't stop it; slang a rock to put money in your pocket.
Blacks—some think to get a part of the dream,
You got to roll by criminal means.
So, Black men, be a man and not a boy.
Be in your child's life—
Not just give them a dollar or a toy.
Bring to their life lots of joy,
Be a father, not just a baby pusher.
If you don't raise your kids,
You're going to wish you had,
Be a dad.

BLACK WOMAN

The Black woman is what I am, was, and will always be—
Sadness and sorrow all around me.
To find a Black man to understand,
Hold my hands, not hit or demand,
To hold me in his arms,
Keep me from all harms.
Men, like the ocean, slowly come, slowly go.
How do men think? Little do I know.
Some are shallow as a puddle,
Yet, some meant nothing, some meant a lot to me.
The Black woman wants a lover, a man, and a friend,
To be here now, forever, and then.
To me, Black sisters shouldn't hit their sisters.
Love their brothers but respect their mothers.
Stop killing each other and live together.
Keep the peace—not for a day, a month, but forever.

GUNSHOT LULLABY

Children die, mothers cry, brothers lie—
Dead, and the thought in my head is, why?
Gunshot lullaby.
Chalk line and the bloodstain,
Gunshot to the head, a bullet in your brain.
Seems everybody's leaving me with a memory,
When I die, I wonder, who will shed a tear for me?
No love from my family or my mama.
As methods bring the pain, I come with the drama—
All drama, with mad agony,
I cannot deny what I see.
All alone, no one there,
Life's like a dream of a thousand nightmares.
In my face as reality stares—
Yes, it stares right in my eye.
Children die, mothers cry, brothers lie—
Dead, and the thought in my head is, why?
Gunshot lullaby.

I'm leaning on the everlasting body in a casket,
Getting sown like flower seeds in the ground as the fertilizer.
And you realize, not just reminisce,
About what you miss.
Tuck away the pain—that's why many scream and cry,
Life gone before a goodbye,
Eternal sleep from the gunshot lullaby.

MY ROBOT

I invent people, see, it's like mental building blocks.
A thief has been committed, so I call the cops.
I've been robbed by my own robot.
I start to pull the plug, but I could not—
After all, I built him this way.
See, wherever we would play in the bed, there I lay—
Just another jewel in his box of jewels.
Love was the laboratory where I built fools,
Just to push a button and play by their rules.
I turn the boiler on, heat it fast,
Pour into the mixing glass.
I created you like a home remedy,
Yet, side effects, temporarily,
I could hear or could see, but finally, it wore off.
Eventually, I could see clear and hear—
Only to find, my lover was a figment of my imagination.
Even during his touch, I still needed emotional, intellectual,
And spiritual masturbation.

How can I be satisfied being 2, 3, or who knows?
His only concern when you come up out of them clothes.
I invented a vibrator with arms, life-like feeling.
Love couldn't just be created because I knew this was real.
After all this time in the lab,
A rejected lover is all I had.
Still, I have not discovered the formula for love...
That's sad!

LIFE BEAUTIFUL SORROWS

The picture, from the scripture,
From the book of life as we live.
Yet, we only take, never give.
We take complete advantage,
No understanding how we manage,
Or how they gave over.
Life's heavy load on my shoulder.
This heavy load, lift it off,
Everyone getting paid, only at my cost.
Respect I lost,
Lost for many, what be the purpose to envy?
To treat one the way you would want to be treated,
Seems not needed in this society.
The question remains, why this be the policy?
Why ideology and stupidity?

Many, if will infest, I manifest, restrain,
My reaction and tactics.
Find relation in the mathematics,
Yet, only Dave Jarred, not Allah,
Because Christ be the one that I follow.
But for many individuals,
It is going to take a miracle,
For me not to become physical and turn the other cheek.
For God loves the humble and meek,
The meek and humble.
Often do I stumble but never fall,
Struggle from Saul to Paul.
For example, it seems many try to trample,
All over me, it is hard to maintain sanity.
So hard do I try to say hello,
But opportunity says goodbye.
Friends become distant, they leave or die.
Every year I shed a tear for the dead,
Every life important, yet nothing done or said. Why?

DO OR DIE

I got to do or die, because I can't live for you and I.
Life as a soldier, all battles I conquer over,
I camouflage my identity,
Close my eyes to the things I don't want to see.
I don't want to see the pain of reality.
My eyes are closed to the situations around me.
So many times, do we ask why?
Why do things happen to the just?
Why is doubt in the God we trust?
Why is the best woman met by the worst man?
Questions often wondered,
But yet, I may never understand.
To live in a fairy tale like Mr. Roger's neighborhood,
Where it's never all good.
If I could, I would make dealers smoke their own shit.
If I could, I would make the crackheads quit.
The children without guidance,
The pothead's closed eyelids.
Don't forget about our kids as we live only for I and I.
Survival of the fittest, either we do or die.

ONE SISTER TO ANOTHER

One sister to another,
I want to speak to provide you with serenity,
For all the things they do to me.
You see, when you go through,
I go through; that's how we do what we do.
You know that you're my sister for sure,
As long as you know, once upon a time,
We were all platinum dimes.
Who didn't take because we spoke our minds,
And would have our girls say, "How you do? (Oh, just fine.)"
Back in the day, we were raised to be my sister's keeper,
Love went beyond blood; it couldn't come no deeper.
Self-love, self-esteem, and respect to you I gave,
I teach my sister from tribulations.
The road was rocky, but for you, I gave.
The path on our love, no one could do the math,
Why? Because it just would not add up.
You are my eagle wings,
Born from the greatest.
Could never be torn apart.
No one could remove them from my heart,
Not Daddy, sister, friend, or lover,
I had to tell, girl, one sister to another.

EYES CLOSED

If I could close my eyes and dream of back then,
Or what used to be,
You would find me no longer wishing for what once was mine.
No longer being pushed aside or behind someone else.
If I could close my eyes and take a breath,
Would I exhale to breathe again?
Only then will I close my eyes to see more clearly.
Closing my eyes helps me to see my reflection in my mental mirror.
I wrote this because my mirror grew out of focus,
Friends no longer meet expectations,
Commitments now lack dedication.
Keys jiggle as I search to find,
The one that turns the doorknob of foreign land,
Greeted by a stranger's hand.
If I could close my eyes,
I hear strange voices speaking gibberish,
That is translated into things that make no sense.
Only to be believed as truth.

YOUR CHANGE

You left a dime and now you don't have a penny.
You feel me, as you were too blind to see me in all my mental riches and I
was golden.
Now, I'm going to see if you do better with those other chick stories
unfolding.
Other mommies might close your eyes if you're looking to find me.
To look for me never again, do I want to be found?
You had me left when in my heart was bound,
Bound and bonded. My heart you were fond to it.
Here's your change, listen to it jingle.
I got the game to mingle when a dime,
And a penny don't make much sense.
You penny player got my heart quick.
It had to be love, because you didn't have anything.
My money, my body, house, car, gas, your food, your clothes.
Only God knows, why—what was I thinking?
Falling in love when in lies, I was sinking.
Now I realize a dime and a penny don't make much sense.
Just don't add up when you don't have a buck, a dollar bill.
How does it feel when the grass isn't greener ?

The well's dry—now you're the one that wonders now.
As you hear the change jingle, see my angle.
Because you left a dime and now you don't have anything but a penny.
Feel me? You changed.

REST MY LOVE

I'm so tired of being in love.
Love so much, I find myself by myself, loving myself.
Love to the point where I have a usual taste for BS.
Having beyond the don't stops, hell, I can't quit.
Loving used to be confusing.
Love loves no one.
Could I be singing the blues?
Love that once had me red as fire.
Brainwashed that I got to have that love, but I'm tired.
My soul grows weary, but it is rejuvenated by my spirit.
God is love, and if I listen to Him, I will hear it.

MAKING MUSIC

Slippery secrets slip out of me every time I ooze on these sheets.
Thoughts tap beats.
He eats Omega's Sweets.
Like chocolate valentines,
Every line is morsels to his mind.
It's hard to be dark chocolate.
Coconut makes you crazy.
I guess that's why I'm still a single lady.
So chocolate, I'm seizure sexy.
He shakes every time he's next to me.
You see, I want to stimulate, but be led to see the mirrors of his mind,
That they magnify shadows of his soul.
Let there be light,
That I might see my reflection in his heart,
While I am walking through walls built with hurt and bricks of pain,
Haiku healing is performing in syllables,
When he says my name.
The Pisces will swim in the legacies of him,
And we make milky melodies of oohs and aahs.
He vibrates my walls with 16 bars.
We make music; if it is a note, we use it.

Omega is the song that never ends.
You hear it every time you see him,
And he recorded my best.
It plays back when I lay on his chest.
My thoughts tap his heartbeats.
We recorded again and again on these sheets.

HOW MANY OF US HAVE, "FRIENDS?"

People make the world go round.

Take a moment and look around.

I've got love for you—once was lost, but again I found.

As I sit back and reflect, you're not perfect,

But my own faults I neglect.

I'm quick to build walls, my heart to protect.

But you gave me something I will always have to respect: a friendship.

Though sometimes I raise my voice out of pain,

My mix compliments while I complain,

But you mean no less—I still love you the same.

As I, why? Friendship.

Though life may trip, sometimes I might flip,

Land on my friend's feelings—may not be fair.

Though I may not say, I do care, because I know you try.

Why? Friendship.

Too many times, I look to you to do what I can't do,

Be a hero, heroine.

But regardless of your shortcomings, my heart is still warm,

Even through differences arose,
To battle life, you and I, God chose.
And even in distance, memories still grow,
About everything, something through God, you bring.

SELF-PROMISE

Many stories never told,
My mind in bondage, yet never captured my soul.
My heart and mind work as one,
Yet, it seems the battle of love for me, I never won.
As you want to cum through the night,
Then it hits—the morning light.
Only to discover, now the cover is empty,
In my time of need but filled once again in your time of pleasure.
You've sampled my gold,
But haven't discovered the hidden treasure.
To my heart, do you have the key?
How do I know it's not he or him?
Too many times have I seen the light of love, yet lust made dim.
Do not ask me to leave my throne as a queen,
To be your temporary hoe—
Do not assume my wants; just ask, and you will know.
With my heart, never again will I play Russian roulette.
No more will I do, to later regret.
My mind is set; promises I'll keep.
Never broken, my promises I've kept.
My body you can't feel if my love you never felt.

MIND OF A CHILD

Growing up too soon, up too fast,
Having a childhood—time won't last.
Coping with the future, trying to handle the past,
Life is short; it only lasts a while.
Mind of a woman or mind of a child.
Babies raising babies, boys being fathers,
This issue is hard to swallow.
Men leaving children because he's a boy
Playing a man's game—it's a shame
When a baby only knows his dad's name.
Life is short; it only lasts a while.
Mind of a woman or mind of a child.
A twenty with a teen, through love,
Share some of the sweetest dreams.
Is he too old for her—or him?
Are their minds ready for an adult relationship and love?
This can only be decided by the God above.
Enjoy life—it's short and only lasts a while.
Mind of a woman or mind of a child.

NOBODY'S CHILD

Nobody cares, anybody there, anybody's child?
Why do I live this lifestyle?
Here is Dad and Mama, here the drama,
The life I live, nothing in the world ever gives.
In this world, I have nothing but self,
As I look around, I see nothing left.
The criminal mind—it's time, and nobody's here,
I learned to keep no one close, no one near.
Dad's been gone since I was three,
I make it on my own in society.
Mama gave me up, she just gave me away,
Tears fill my eyes, searching for a better day.
A head full of anger, love from strangers,
Many say, "It's time to let go and move on."
But what they don't know—it's easier said than done.
How can they tell me how to deal with my pain,
When in my heart, I know they've felt the same?
I've shed so many tears for the years I've been here,
No one on this earth but God, I fear.
Why do we cry? Tears do nothing to help.
Troubles of life—I've learned to expect.

Through social services, I plead my case,
Moving from place to place, just another face.
They see me, but I'm nothing to them—
Making it on my own in this society is grim.
Trouble doesn't last always, but it stays a while.
Nobody cares, nobody's there, nobody's child.
Why do I live this hellish lifestyle?

CUT OFF

"I love you," don't sell tickets to the next BS show,
No need to gather 'round to see how far he will go,
Move the spotlight to showcase another hoe.
You didn't know? I will cut you off like an ingrown toenail,
Or other stuff that irritates me.
Even a blind man could see—I am not the one,
If you want to play dumb, I'll be your Special Ed teacher,
Here's a finger if you need sign language to reach you.
I'll meet you at the door to choke ignorance out of your throat,
"Baby, baby, please," in the **Key of bum** note.
Your lies may have made me float,
But reality keeps me grounded,
Common sense? I found it.
Between the whys and goodbyes,
It makes sense why you think I won't say goodbye—
Because I haven't yet,
But I refuse to take another moment of regret.

You've been charged with:
Reckless endangerment of my mind,
Assault on my soul,
First-degree murder of our trust—
And you kidnapped "us."
Where are you taking us? What is this place?
By the look on your face, his face, the past face,
This was a bittersweet taste—
Of sweet-and-sour mess served with some dumb hoe.
Pass my chopsticks,
This is another takeout order,
Check, please!

JUST ANOTHER NUMBER

Free, like at last—
Slaves of the past reincarnate in orange jumpsuits,
Or black leather combat boots,
Just an endless pursuit to be free.
She wanted to go home—GI 254318283,
She wanted to go home—inmate 254318283,
They seem the same to me.
Soldiers fight for freedom of speech,
But are not allowed to speak,
Or think alone.
This is BS—America's fundraiser.
She pays herself very well.
And like Vickie,
She has a secret she will never tell:
The military bottom hoe.
They don't need to know—
Just do what you're told,
America's fundraiser: souls for gold.
Pieces for pain, stacks for straight,
Luxuries for life.

A 2-for-1 sale:
Military hoes and civilians are the best,
I get the check first,
And give them the rest.
I rest in relief—
Relaxation releases freedom in pieces.
Peace in piece:
Part pursuit, profit purchase, progression—
For the price of a life's lesson,
I want to be free.
I fight to be free.
Free from optical illusions,
Looks like drawing collisions.
Free to go, come, move, and shake,
Give and take, build, break, add, subtract,
Sit still.
Limitless—
No boundaries, no borders,
No commands or orders.
No settling, mess-starting, meddling,
Telling me nothing to do.

UNKNOWN MELODY

Am I just another lady that sings the blues?
Singing out of key or is this just an unknown melody I sing?
I know many who sing the blues every time they play the game.
Some play for fortune and fame,
And some are still playing for love—it's a shame.
Things have changed;
Now love is the game of fools.
Those who play to win,
Only win a chance to lose.
Many may laugh but just do the math—
For how many tears shed,
How your heart has bled,
Every time I was misled.
Lies have paralyzed.
Cupid got me stupid, love got me sprung,
It's the 4th quarter, and I still haven't won.
'Cause I'm just another lady singing the blues.
Singing out of key,
Or is love just an unknown melody?

WHAT ABOUT OUR OWN?

Diversity led me to the reality,
That unity could never be.
When morality crashed into sociality,
It became the fatality of peace.
Rage, rage into the dying of the light—
We gotta fight.
Fight for what now?
I'm stuck seeing soldiers in combat boots.
Numerous banners read, "We support our troops,"
But to do what now?
I'm stuck watching sons snatched from fathers,
Mothers from daughters.
Families torn apart at the government's order,
To bring peace through bullets,
And new life through many deaths.
Jesus wept—we saw His passion,
In God we trust to create assassins.
To kill, kill for freedom.
Is the battle truly to be won?
When Saddam lives unscathed,
And SPC Jones becomes just another cost.

Administratively, we pop corks of champagne,
While our leaders become intoxicated,
Unable to see our pain.
Here we are—
Homeless, jobless,
But told, "God bless."
Our troops wear combat boots in a foreign man's land,
While rejected by their own.

LOVE IS BLIND

A reflection throws back what you see.
A joke is supposed to be funny,
But how can I look in the mirror at God's creation,
And not like what I see?
If life's a joke, then why am I laughing so little?
Mirror, mirror, on my wall,
I smash you, throw you away,
Break you into little pieces,
Crush glass under my feet.
What truth is in the truth I seek?
You look in my mirror and say, "Ugly,"
But perfection in you, I do not see.
In no one's reflection is their perfection,
Yet, you never make a self-confession.
The world is so torn up, and we're doing it—
From friendships to relationships, drugs, and shit.
To love is to die and to live is to cry.

Why do we cry?
Are tears magic droplets that wash the pain away?
Can all the anger, the pain, the hurt,
Stream from my face where tears flow—
Is pain in place?
Why do we need people?
We meet them every day,
And over and over again, they mess up our lives.
The more we try, the more we die inside,
Wrapped in lies.
Ok, stab so hard that we find
We start over again.
Why do we need love?
We do the friend or dating dance,
And what happens?
We're happy, we hunt for happier—
The more we hurt.
So why do I live, searching for that happy moment,
Only to have it taken?
Why, every time, is love mistaken,
For weakness?
But revenge—
Revenge is life's sweetness.

WHY DO YOU DO ME THIS WAY?

Why did you do me this way?
When I ask what's wrong, nothing you say.
How could you leave me and not say goodbye,
As I cry out, why?
Choice—I choose a mother's love, I lose.
Holding me tight, saying it will be alright.
She brought me into this world,
Then left me alone.
The pain I feel is you being gone.
Waking up in the morning, getting ready for school,
I thank you for teaching me life's rule.
I remember how you held out your hand,
Made me understand God's perfect plan.
My heart is wiped with pain as you remain gone.
All I ever wanted was a mother to call my own.
Blood is thicker than water; no one can take your place.
I have her eyes, and I've got my mother's face.

Where are you now? Where have you been?
You weren't just a mother—you were my best friend.
In your place, there will be no one.
Now it's time to say, what's done is done.
Through my God, choice—I choose a mother's love, lose.
Dear Mama, no matter what you have done, or I have done,
I love you, I miss you, I wish you were here.
I will love you, distance or near.
There is nothing but God that could come first,
Like a real mother.
So, God, please give her back to me.

YOUR LOVE I LOSE

Why did you do me this way?
When I ask you what is wrong, *nothing*, you would say.
How could you leave me and never say goodbye?
I ask why, as the tears fall from my eyes.
Choice—I choose your love I lose.
Holding me tight, saying everything would be alright.
You gave me the world, and then you left me all alone.
The pain I feel since you've been gone—
Waking up in the morning with my eye on you.
In this world, there's nothing I can do
To have you come back to me.
How can I make you see my pain?
When you left me, I saw a storm and felt the rain.
My heart is wrapped with pain as you remain gone.
You gave me someone to call my own.
I long to touch your smooth face—
In my heart, no one can take your place.

I know it's too late, but I'll admit the mistake.
To say what is done is done.
In your place, there is no one.
I apologize for the choices I choose.
I miss you—your love I lose.

TIME TO LOVE SELF

My heart feels like every second I'm fighting to love you,
And every second I'm fighting not to love you.
My heart splits, running away from my mind,
Which screams, what I should do?
My heart runs from my mind,
Yelling justifications—why I should stay, why I should leave?
We talk until I believe this is for me.
Chasing love is the carrot; loneliness is the string.
I can't wait to see what happiness brings.
The ones you love the most hurt you the worst.
I don't want him. I don't want to want him.
Yet, I can't get you out of my system.
Daily, I practice being dumb.
My reality doesn't make sense.
I just want to get off this fence.
I want to move on, but I keep coming back—
Broken promises tied to the way you act.

Your love is like a cavity—
The sweeter you are, the more it decays me.
Every second I'm with you,
I move an hour away from myself.
Every minute I think of you,
I lose my breath, simply wishing I'd let go.

WEATHER OR NOT

The clouds moved into my life, casting an overcast.
My sunlight taken away, I could not see the path.
Whether man gave warning, for me, they went unheeded.
The rain made my garden sprout but with more weeds in it.
It began to drizzle, and I just looked at the drop and drip.
Life began to flip; mine started to trip.
Ashamed of the game, pride sealed my lips,
Still watching the drop and the drip.
Then the floodgates opened, and I began to drown,
Trying to sip what I thought was reality.
Caught wrong, searching for my umbrella in a fellow,
Only to be lied to and left out in the cold.
It took many years before I found shelter in my soul,
A self-light bright as sunshine, worth more than gold.
Daily, I grab my pen for my sun rays to come in,
As my story unfolds and tomorrow becomes a new day
With the possibility of rain.
Now, I embrace the drip and the drop,
As it washes away my pain.

RELATED TO MY ENEMIES

Family became my worst enemy.
Don't remember me when I'm doing better.
No matter—hear the chick cheddar lies in the light, people scatter.
To question me brings no answer, envious cancer,
As I try to make my paper.
Why do people want to hate you?
Same blood, thicker than water—why bother?
When friends come before family, but in the end,
Family is there in a time of need.
But you don't remember back then,
When Mike needed shoes, who was there to do?
You're doing fine, so you forgot me,
Now talking about me like you're a juvenile.
Makes me say, "Ooh, child, when are things going to get easier?"
When the world keeps getting greedier.
Glad to meet you, so I can give you the picture.
It's in the scripture—
In the last days, mother against daughter, father against son.
Daily, I see it done.

My family, I let go; I let them be.
Damn shame, family turned into an enemy.
I shake them haters off, and I'm going to do me.

I CAN MAKE IT

I can make it.
I might be a mistake, but I've got what it takes,
'Cause I can make it.
Nothing's given to me in this world—it's up to me to take it,
I reiterate, I might be my mama's mistake.
But there's no need to wallow in my own self-pity.
I'm on a mission, state to state, around the world, city to city.
Getting what I need without charity,
I'll succeed, even if I'm alone, left standing,
Whether I have to be assertive or demanding.
I'm a go-getter, chasing the cheddar and cream.
I can't help it—I've got a dollar-dollar dream.
Making a dollar, my pride, I'll never swallow.
Mama might have made a mistake, Daddy neglected,
Society rejected, but I chase money, so you've got to respect it.
Respect me—even my enemies can see,
I've got those dollar-dollar dreams.
I look in the mirror. I might see my mama's mistake,
But I've got what it takes.
I can make it.

I'VE BEEN ROBBED

Life's like a box of chocolates,
Daily, I taste its bitter sweetness,
Over the years, it seems love's been a weakness.
In love, it's a thin line between truth and stupidity.
You trust the truth only to be lied to.
Life's like a box of chocolates—
You never know what you're going to get into.
As I wonder why, should I keep tasting or quit?
Is it worth the search, worth the hurt?
Distracted from reality, I gotta get my senses alert.
How could the sweetest thing I ever known,
Be the one I hate since the day you were gone?
I've been robbed—where is the justice for a broken heart?
Emergency, emergency, 911,
I would like to report what you have done.
My feelings are damaged, tears are missing, and my heart is broken,
A crime committed every time three words are spoken.
Why did you do it? *Robbery* is now a mystery—case unsolved.
Somebody tell me, where is the justice for a broken heart?

Larceny, my prized possession has been stolen,
I've been robbed—emergency, emergency, 911.
Somebody listen, I want to report what you have done.
This may not be the last time,
But sadly, I must say,
This was not the first time I've been robbed.

IF SHE COULD HEAR ME

I want to put it down, just open my mouth and have folk memorize,
Words coming out of my mouth, having them hypnotized.
My tongue swings like a pendulum, back and forth,
Taking you on a verbal journey—verse, set our course.
We go deeper than the ocean's depth,
Verbs, nouns, and pronouns so profound,
It's like scriptures—Jesus wept.
Got you thinking, if He's seeing, should He still be weeping?
Martha should still be mourning.
Little girl to grown, and she wears high-heeled shoes,
Little girl paying a grown woman's dues,
Because she chose to spread her legs open and give birth to despair.
Meanwhile, little boys want to be men, but Daddy's not there.
She reaches for the pacifier to hush away the static,
Screams rocking despair, she reaches for the blanket,
Wipes him tightly in what should have been her self-esteem.
For it seems scattered dreams came when I saw her eyeliner, lipstick, and
blush.
She rushes her innocence away and had no time for child's play.
So these are not nursery rhymes,
Only a mark in time, where we lose ourselves.

CALLING ALL POETS, THE WHOLE WORLD NEEDS US!

This is my thesis, hypothesis, or just a guess.
I remember back in the days when we were poets.
Back in the days, all we wanted was to be heard,
And didn't really care if we were seen.
Mic fiend, just needed the mic.
When all we could think about was what to write for me and let you see,
My tears in the shadows, thongs in my bedroom,
Thoughts that walk a tightrope,
Passes pens that scramble for hope,
My sheets speak to the broken-hearted.
She did me wrong to the day I met you, poets.
Calling all poets, the whole world needs us.
Like back in the days when backpacks and notebooks

were sexy at open mic nights.
The veterans would encourage the closet poets to share.
Now they only care about whose Bic is bigger than yours,
Sheets slipperier than yours.
Poets messing up the art I love.
No longer do we inspire but just hire actors and pretenders.
Are you Langston or LL Cool J?
Are you Cannabis, sending a message, or hot air blowing hot pieces
That warm the hearts of no one?
Once upon a time, when we taught, reached, and preached what we lived.
Poets.
If I forgot my line, it's cool.
I'm not an actor.
I don't have a punchline.
I'm not a rapper.
If I bore you, I couldn't give a lovely damn.
I'm not an entertainer. I am a *poet*.
The days of Sis. Journey's love song to Forressa's Grove,
My Cocofire knew a hard rain was coming,
because Chris saw lightning in the sky.
After Bee would see the wind blow,
We were a family with group pieces,
And our solo showed me he still loves his sisters.
Calling all poets, the whole world needs you.

HIS NAME

God's anger will not hold forever,
Come as you are, but don't leave the same,
Let your life not keep mocking His name.
Churches, stop accepting sin,
Stop making excuses to do it over and over again.
He knows my heart, He does have mercy on our soul,
But if we don't repent, our heart won't be clean.
Bitter and sweet can't be.
Be a light, and darkness will flee.
Who is your daddy?
What cup do you drink?
As a man thinks, so he must be — pure, lovely, and just.
Is it God you trust or your hustle?
By Your might, Lord, or my own muscle, will I fail?
Our mind is blind, and we've forgotten the nails that built the church,
If we don't want God now, then He doesn't want us later.
God sees us in the shadows. He's looking, and one day,
His reward will be with Him.

If you can't lie, use it, abuse it, drink it, smoke it, cuss it, fuss it,
In heaven, why do it now?
Holy Spirit, can these dry bones live?
I speak life over the dead.
Sin is death — no more unclean spirits, break every chain.
You may come as you are but don't leave the same.
We can't keep living where we mock the Most High God's name.

MY X

I chase chocolate-covered rainbows,
But in the end, there is no pot of gold.
I ride psychedelic unicorns,
But in the end, the harness breaks.
I chase dreams, but I have made some mistakes,
Like that one mistake that changed my name,
It changed my life,
No longer was I, Omega McNeal, sit still,
New name: Inmate 169318.
They couldn't wait, trapped between generational X and Y,
I've been every X and don't know why.
You know, x-addict, x-con, x-wife, and x-girl.
In your world, all you could see is an **X**.
Life has been hard, so I've taken it hit after hit.
Many wonder how I became the alcoholic, weed head, powder puff girl.
In your world, all you can see is an **X**.

I could never understand, for the life of me,
Why did I pay my debt to society?
Only to get out and tell everyone I was in,
On every application I fill in.
Were you convicted? Were you convicted?
No, I'm *convinced*,
That when you couldn't see a person,
After losing my kids, my cars, my house, and even my sanity,
God could *still* see the best in me.
This is not a poem, but my testimony of Yah and Amen.

OMEGA'S GUMBO

Menu for Your Mind, to Stir Up Your Soul, Life has many flavors,
And this is just a taste of Omega.
I thank God for all my struggles that seasoned me.
My trials tenderized my heart,
And my challenges cooked my courage to perfection.
This could only be possible by making Christ my head chef.
He has put many in my path, and I give a special thanks to:
First, God;
My husband, Nate McNeal;
My daughters, Divine & Wisdom Alice, Island Riley, and Tatiyona
McNeal;
My family and friends; Beyond the Veil Family;
Welcome To The Storm Publishing; The Hungry Poets; Coach Carter;
And fellow poets and artists.
I truly hope at least one, if not all, of these poems touch,
educate, or inspire you in some way.

ABOUT THE AUTHOR

Omega McNeal is a dedicated wife, mother, Army veteran, and community volunteer who brings passion, integrity, and purpose to every role she undertakes. Her real estate journey began in 2005 as an office coordinator in property management and consulting. Driven by a deep commitment to serve others, she became a licensed real estate agent in 2019 and has since helped countless individuals and families navigate the path to homeownership.

With 11 years of honorable military service, Omega gained the discipline, resilience, and leadership skills that continue to shape her professional and personal life. Her commitment to service didn't end with the Army—she continues to support fellow veterans as a devoted volunteer at the DAV 29 service office.

In addition to her work in real estate and veteran advocacy, Omega has been active in ministry for over 17 years, offering spiritual guidance and encouragement to those in need. Her diverse background allows her to connect with people from all walks of life and serve her community with empathy and excellence.

For Omega McNeal, every story is a journey, and success is the path she walks with purpose and heart.

ACKNOWLEDGEMENTS

I thank God for all my struggles that have seasoned me. My trials have tenderized my heart, and my challenges have cooked my courage to perfection. This could only be possible by making Christ my Head Chef.

He has placed many wonderful people in my path, and I give special thanks first to my Lord and Savior, Jesus Christ. To my husband, Nate McNeal; Divine and Wisdom Alice; Island Riley and Tatiyona McNeal, my daughters; my family; my church family; my friends; Welcome To The Storm Publishing; The Hungry Poets; Coach Carter; fellow poets and artists; and last but not least, all my haters — I thank you.

I truly hope that at least one, if not all, of these poems will touch, educate, or inspire you in some way.